SAURUS STREET

A Pterodactyl Stole My Homework

Nick Falk and Tony Flowers

RANDOM HOUSE AUSTRALIA

For the terrifying Murgasaurs – Adam, Luke and Olivia
– Nick Falk

For Josh and Tallis, my pair of pterodactyl chasers
– Tony Flowers

A Random House book
Published by Random House Australia Pty Ltd
Level 3, 100 Pacific Highway, North Sydney NSW 2060
www.randomhouse.com.au

First published by Random House Australia in 2013

Addresses for companies within the Random House Group can be found at
www.randomhouse.com.au/offices

National Library of Australia
Cataloguing-in-Publication Entry

Author: Falk, Nicholas
Title: A pterodactyl stole my homework / Nick Falk; Tony Flowers, Illustrator
ISBN: 978 1 74275 656 1 (pbk)
Series: Falk, Nicholas. Saurus street; 2
Target Audience: For primary school age
Subjects: Pterodactylidae – Juvenile fiction
Other Authors/Contributors: Flowers, Tony
Dewey Number: A823.4

Cover and internal illustrations by Tony Flowers
Internal design and typesetting by Anna Warren, Warren Ventures
Printed in Australia by Griffin Press, an accredited ISO AS/NZS 14001:2004 Environmental
Management System printer

Random House Australia uses papers that are natural, renewable and recyclable products and made from wood grown in sustainable forests. The logging and manufacturing processes are expected to conform to the environmental regulations of the country of origin.

CHAPTER ONE

An Unexpected Visitor

Tap tap tap.

There's someone knocking on my window. Which is weird, because my room's in the attic. I listen, but I can't hear a thing. Except for Mr Tiblins's **snoring**. (Mr Tiblins lives two

1

doors up the road from us. He's the loudest snorer on Saurus Street.)

I creep to the window. I'm pretty scared. I hope there isn't something out there. Like a face with blood-red eyes. But I bet there is.

I peek through the curtains. Nothing. Just the night. Still pretty scary. But at least there are no **monsters**.

I go back to my desk. I'm doing my homework and I need to finish it. Otherwise I'll be in big trouble. That's what Mum said. And she wasn't joking. Mum never jokes.

I'm writing about pterodactyls. That's my homework. To write two pages about my favourite dinosaur. And my favourite dinosaurs are pterodactyls. *Ter-Oh-Dac-Tils*. Even though they're not actually dinosaurs. They're pterosaurs. *Ter-Oh-Saws*. You don't pronounce the Ps. They're just stuck on the front for fun.

Pterodactyls were the biggest flying animals ever. They were **huge**. And they were meat eaters, like eagles and hawks are today. Except pterodactyls hunted dinosaurs. I'd like to see an eagle take on a dinosaur. It'd have no chance.

It's taken me all weekend to do this homework. It's **brilliant**.

I've even done pictures. Like this one. It's a picture of a pterodactyl fighting oviraptors. Oviraptor means egg thief in Latin, which is a language people use to name dinosaurs.

Oviraptors liked eating pterodactyl eggs. They reckoned they tasted great, like chocolate. So pterodactyls used to fight them, to stop them stealing their eggs. Fair enough, really.

Tap **tap** *tap.*

There it is again. A knocking on my window. I hold my breath and listen. Silence. But I definitely heard it.

This is bad news. I'm all alone up here. Mum and my brother Nathan are downstairs watching TV. And downstairs is miles away. If I scream, the thing outside will eat me. Mum and Nathan will be too late.

I could try hiding, but it won't work. Whatever it is will find me. Monsters always do.

I'm going to have to look.

I tiptoe back to the window. My

heart's beating really fast, like a drum. I take a deep breath. Then I open the curtains – quickly, before I lose my nerve.

And there it is.

A big black shadow.

With wings and claws and blood-red eyes. It's come to eat me.

I jump back from the window. The monster raises a claw. It pushes on the glass. It's not locked! The window's opening! I'm done for.

I look around for a weapon. All I can find is a plastic light saber. It'll have to do.

I adopt the Jedi stance. This will be Sam Smith's last stand.

The window opens.

The monster leaps into the room.

6

It's enormous! It's got a huge crest and giant wings and sharp spiky teeth. It opens its mouth. It's about to **ATTACK!**

And . . . and . . . and . . . the monster squawks.

SQUAWK!

And that's when I realise. It's not a monster. It's a pterodactyl. A real live pterodactyl. And it's standing in my bedroom.

8

CHAPTER TWO
The Homework Thief

Mum's gonna have a fit. I'm not allowed friends in my room after dark. And I reckon that includes pterosaurs.

The pterodactyl starts hopping round my room. It's **massive**. Its crest is touching the ceiling, and if it opened its wings they'd touch both walls.

But what's it doing in my bedroom?

Pterodactyls lived in the Cretaceous period, which was ages ago. And it's the Holocene period now. And the Holocene period doesn't have pterosaurs. Or dinosaurs. Or any other sort of saurs.

Maybe I made it with my imagination. I've been imagining pterodactyls all weekend. Maybe I imagined a bit too hard.

The pterodactyl keeps on hopping. It's looking for something. Maybe it's hungry? I offer it the rest of my banana but it's not interested. What's it after then?

Oh.

My homework.

The pterodactyl hops over to my desk. Maybe it wants to check if I got my facts right?

10

Or maybe not. The pterodactyl picks up my homework and hops to the window. It's going to steal it. And that would be a **DISASTER**. Mum'll murder me if I lose my homework. That'll be five lost homeworks in a row.

'Give that back,' I say. I grab the homework and pull. But the pterodactyl's having none of it. It lets out a mighty squawk, opens its wings and flies out the window . . . taking me with it.

WHOA!

I've always wanted to fly. I've even tried making cardboard wings, but they never work. Well, now I'm doing it. And I can tell you one thing, it's not as relaxing as it looks.

sWOOP!

The pterodactyl dives over the garden.

WHOOSH!

It zooms over the fence. Both my slippers fall off, straight into Jack's garden. His dog Charlie will probably eat them, which is a shame because I liked those slippers. They had dragons on them.

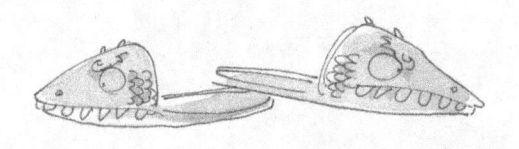

We start flying higher. It's lucky school paper is tough, otherwise I'd be a goner. I'm holding on to one end of my homework. The pterodactyl's got the other. One rip and I'll become a Sam pancake.

I give the homework one last pull but it's no use. The pterodactyl's not letting go. And I'm about to go **SPLAT**.

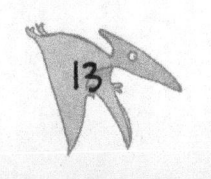

13

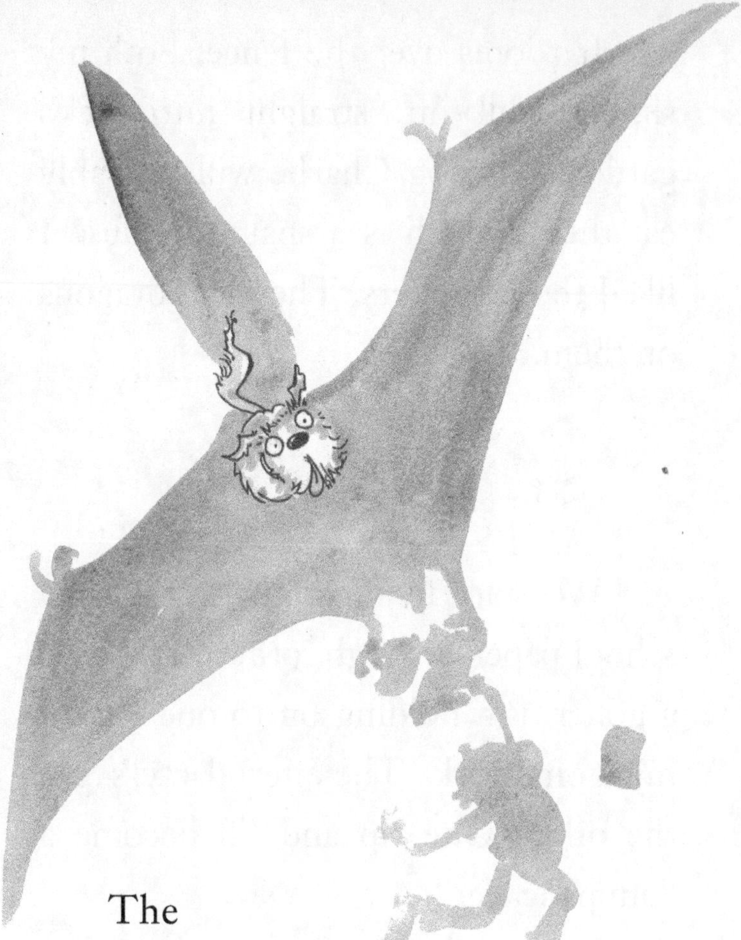

The
pterodactyl's
aiming straight for
a telegraph pole. I think it's
trying to get rid of me.

14

I look down. Road. That's what's beneath me. And it's not very soft.

But hang on. What's that? It's a bush! That should be soft. I wait till we're over it. Then I let go.

AAAIIIEEEE!

I fall through the sky.

THUNK

I land in the bush. A direct hit.

Pity it's a thornbush. I get a bum full of prickles.

I tumble out of the bush. My pyjamas are ripped, I'm covered in cuts and I'm freezing. But that's not the worst of it. The worst thing is losing my homework. I'm in **serious trouble**. Mum'll be furious.

15

And as for Miss Potts . . . I don't even want to think about it.

I look up. There goes the pterodactyl. Flying up towards the **clouds**. I'll never see that homework again. And there's no way I can redo it. It took me ages.

I'm just going to have to try telling the truth.

CHAPTER THREE
Team Dinosaur

'A *what?*'

Mum's face is bright red. She's about to **explode**.

'A pterodactyl,' I repeat.

'It's an extinct flying reptile,' says my brother Nathan. 'Era – Late Cretaceous, Order – Pterosauria.'

'I know what it is!' snaps Mum.

Nathan returns to his cornflakes.

'And I'm supposed to believe this, am I?' Mum asks.

I attempt a reply, but nothing comes out.

'Just like last week? When you said Bertie ate your homework?'

Bertie did eat it. I spilt jam on it. Bertie loves jam.

'And the week before it was the mice!'

They nibbled a hole in my bag. The homework must have fallen out.

'And what was it the week before that?'

'Seagulls,' says Nathan. 'Latin name – Larus.'

'Exactly!' shouts Mum. 'Seagulls!'

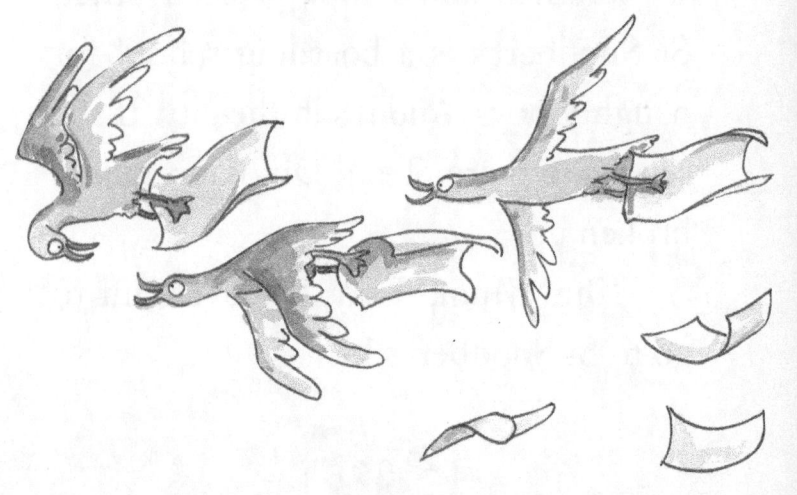

I'm not certain it was seagulls. But that time I dropped some fries on my homework. So I reckon it was.

Mum starts washing the dishes. Violently. The dishes look **nervous**. 'What's your teacher going to say?' she mutters.

I'm trying not to think about that.

'I'm warning you, Sam, this is your last chance. If I get one more call from Miss Potts, then that's it. I'm sending you to St Snodbert's.'

Nathan and I look at each other. St Snodbert's is a boarding school for naughty boys. And it's in the city. If she sends me there, Team Dinosaur will be broken up.

'But, Mum,' I say, 'I don't want to go to St Snodbert's.'

Mum spins around. Her face looks like a big red tomato. **'Then do your homework!'**

She storms out of the room.

'Whoops,' says Nathan.

We watch Mum stomp down the passage.

'Not your finest hour,' he says.

'I know,' I reply.

'Why didn't you just do the homework?'

'I did do it.'

'Then where is it?'

'I told you,' I say, 'a pterodactyl took it.'

Nathan gives me his One Eyebrow Look. 'Are you making up stories?'

'No, I'm not,' I say. 'I don't do that anymore. I'm eight.'

And that's true. I am eight. Nathan's twelve. Four years older. Together we're Team Dinosaur. We build dinosaurs, draw dinosaurs and play dinosaurs.

'Tell me, what did this pterodactyl look like?' Nathan opens his invisible

22

notebook. He's in **_detective_**
mode.

'Big. Two wings, a tail and a crest.'

'Number of claws?'

'Three. On each wing.'

'On the end of the wing or the middle?'

'Middle.'

'How many sets of teeth?'

'Two.'

Nathan narrows his eyes. 'You're serious, aren't you?'

'Of course I'm serious. I never joke about dinosaurs.'

Nathan nods, satisfied. 'Good,' he says. 'Neither do I.' He closes his notebook.

We sit and think for a minute.

'What are we gonna do?' I say.

Nathan's the ideas man. He's in charge of Team Dinosaur. He's Captain. But I'm second in charge. And second in charge isn't bad.

Nathan gives me his **serious** look. 'We're gonna get your homework back. That's what we're gonna do.'

Sounds like a plan. But first of all I've got to survive school.

And that might not be as easy as it sounds.

CHAPTER FOUR
Miss Potts

Miss Potts

'We have a homework thief among us.' Miss Potts prowls between the desks, her huge nose sniffing.

'Billy Thomson.' She jabs a bony finger at Billy.

Billy quivers.

'Homework stolen Friday night. Pinched off his pillow.' She points at Susie. 'Susan Williams.'

25

Susie **shivers**.

'Homework stolen yesterday. Snatched from a schoolbag. Wendy Miller.' She folds a crooked claw over Wendy's shoulder.

Wendy *winces*.

'Homework stolen this morning. Ferreted out of a homework folder. The question is . . . who and where is the thief?' She narrows her eyes and peers at each of us in turn.

This is brilliant. I'm not the only one. I put my hand up. Usually that's a **dangerous** thing to do with Miss Potts. But I'm feeling confident.

Miss Potts eyes me with distaste. Like she's spotted dog poo in the corner. Miss Potts doesn't like me much.

'Yes?' she snaps.

'My homework was stolen too.' I feel hopeful. Surely she'll believe me this time?

'I see,' she says. 'That's very convenient. And when exactly was this?'

'Last night. About nine. And what's more, I saw the thief.'

Miss Potts narrows her eyes.

'Did you indeed. And who was it?'

'It was . . . it was . . .'

'*Yesss?*' **hisses** Miss Potts.

Everyone's looking at me. Suddenly I don't feel quite so confident.

'It was a pterodactyl,' I whisper.

There's silence for a few seconds. And then the whole class starts laughing.

Miss Potts smiles. Unpleasantly. She starts creeping towards me.

'I see,' she says. 'And I suppose Mr Thomson here was robbed by a tyrannosaurus. And Miss Miller by a triceratops.'

She stops right in front of me, her beady eyes fixed on mine.

'I suppose we have dinosaurs running rampant all over Saurus Street?'

She leans closer. 'You, boy, are a nasty little liar.'

'I'm not!' I say.

'And not only are you a liar, but you're lazy. You're the laziest boy I've ever met.' She straightens up and looks around the class. 'The rest of you. You're all excused from homework this week. And if anyone catches our homework thief, there'll be no homework for a month!'

The class **cheers**.

She turns back to me. 'And as for you, I want to see your homework *before* class tomorrow morning.' She leans

29

closer again. Her hairy mole tickles my cheek. 'And if I don't, I'll be on the phone to your mother faster than you

can say St Snodbert's.' She smiles again. Her **twisted** yellow teeth leer at me.

Team Dinosaur is in serious trouble.

CHAPTER FIVE
Algebra

'You could just redo your homework,' suggests Nathan.

'No,' I say. I'm blowing up balloons. It's 8pm. Mum's downstairs watching TV. Mr Tiblins is snoring. And I'm going on a pterodactyl hunt. 'If I redo it, everyone will think I lied.'

'So what?' says Nathan. 'At least you won't get sent to St Snodbert's.'

'I'm fed up with being called a liar,' I say. 'I'm going to catch the thief and bring back proof. Then Miss Potts will have to say sorry. And so will Mum.'

I'm pretty upset. **I never lie.** It's so unfair. It's not my fault bad things keep happening to me.

I climb out my window and clamber up onto the roof. Nathan follows.

'So you're going to follow it?' Nathan asks.

'Yes,' I say.

'Using balloons?'

'Yes.'

Nathan smiles. 'An excellent plan,' he says. He heads back through the window.

I start tying balloons to myself. I've already tied my shoelaces to the chimney to stop me flying off too early.

'I prepared these earlier.' Nathan's back. He hands me a pair of cardboard wings and a crest made out of a cereal box. 'Tie it to your head,' he says.

'What for?'

'As a disguise, silly. And we'll be needing this.' He holds up some paper.

'What is it?'

'Algebra homework.'

I'm a bit confused. 'What's algebra?'

'Maths,' says Nathan, 'using letters instead of numbers.' He leans closer. 'It's used by astronauts.'

'But what's it for?' I ask.

'Bait,' says Nathan. 'Why else would the pterodactyl come back? It wants homework. And this homework's the best there is.'

He starts blowing up balloons and tying them to his arms.

'Are you coming too?' I say.

'Of course,' he says. 'We're Team Dinosaur. We work together.'

We tie on our wings and crests. We sticky-tape the homework to the chimney. And then we wait.

It doesn't take long.

Ten minutes later I see a black shadow, just below the clouds.

'I told you this homework was good,' whispers Nathan.

We wait, fingers on our shoelaces. Ready to pull.

Here comes the pterodactyl. Flying **lower and lower.**

It's magnificent. Its huge wings

35

almost block out the moon.

'Any moment now,' whispers Nathan.

We get ready.

The pterodactyl swoops down towards us.

SNATCH!

It grabs the homework, flaps its wings and starts heading towards the clouds.

'NOW!' shouts Nathan.

We pull on the shoelaces and we're

free! *Up we go!*

For about two seconds. And then we start falling. Straight towards the frog pond.

'Oh dear,' says Nathan. He's not wrong. We're about to get very wet. 'Try flapping,' he shouts.

Yes. Of course. The wings! I flap. But I don't go up. I try flapping harder. I flap and flap and flap. I flap for all I'm worth. But it's no use. Cardboard wings are useless.

Here comes the frog pond. Closer and **closer**. I close my eyes and wait for it.

KER-SPLASH!

Slimy water right up my pants. Team Dinosaur has failed.

38

CHAPTER SIX
Invisible Ink

We drag ourselves out of the pond. We're wet, smelly and **soggy**.

We watch the pterodactyl fly away. Up through the clouds and towards the top of Saurus Hill.

What do we do now? No-one's ever climbed Saurus Hill. There are steep cliffs on every side, and the top is

always hidden by the clouds.
No-one even knows what's up there.

'Hot air,' says Nathan.

'What?'

'Hot air. That's what we need.'

I've no idea what he's on about. I start plucking tadpoles out of my socks.

Nathan grabs my arm. 'It's how hot-air balloons work. The hot air makes them go up. That's why *our* balloons didn't go up. The air wasn't **hot** enough.'

He's got a point. 'But where are we going to get hot air from?'

We have a think. It's super quiet. All we can hear is Mr Tiblins snoring away as usual.

40

'That's it!' shouts Nathan. 'Mr Tiblins! Mum says he's *full* of hot air!'

Mr Tiblins is a champion snorer. Once he snored so loudly a chimney fell off. And it wasn't even his own. If there was snoring in the Olympics, he'd win the gold medal, hands down. There's only one problem. How do you catch a snore?

Nathan smiles. 'I think I've got a plan.'

We sneak into Mr Tiblins's front garden. It's completely **OVERGROWN**.

Thistles and stinging nettles everywhere. Mr Tiblins doesn't like kids much. Once I kicked a ball over his

41

fence. He threw it back over. But not before he'd stabbed it with a garden fork.

We tiptoe round the house to the back door. That's where the cat flap is. And I can fit through cat flaps because I'm super skinny.

42

'Right,' says Nathan. 'On with the invisible ink.' Nathan takes a bottle out of his backpack.

We both take a brush and get painting. First our legs **disappear**. Then our arms. Then our tummies. Soon we're just a pair of floating heads.

'Let's go,' whispers Nathan. I crouch down and squeeze through the cat flap. I have to suck in my tummy because it's a tight fit. But I get through.

'Now open the door,' whispers Nathan.

I reach up to turn the key. But then I hear something. A terrible noise. A frightful grumbling, rumbling noise. The whole room starts to **shudder** and **shake**. It sounds like the growling belly of some hideous monster.

It's coming to get me!

'It's just a snore,' says Nathan. 'Quick, open up.'

He's right. Wow. What a snore!

I turn the key. Nathan's head floats inside. We tiptoe down the passage, towards the living room. That's where the snores are coming from.

44

'Inventory check,' whispers Nathan. 'Straws?'

'Check.'

'Sticky tape?'

'Check.'

'String?'

'Check.'

'Giant balloons?'

'Check.'

'Mission Kidnap Snore is Go!'

Suddenly something *sprints* across the dark passage.

I stifle a yelp.

But it's just a cat. And that's when I remember.

Mr Tiblins doesn't own just one cat. He owns hundreds. He's the CRAZY cat man.

CHAPTER SEVEN
Snore Power

The living room's a MESS. Clothes on the table, sauce on the curtains, rubbish on the floor. There's even a bit of toast stuck to the ceiling. With cheese.

We look around the room. There's no sign of Mr Tiblins. But I tell you what there is. Cats. Loads of 'em.

And they're all in a big pile on the couch. It's like a cat mountain. They look as if they're clinging onto something. But I'm not sure what. Maybe it's an ogre.

Suddenly the cat mountain starts to **shudder** and **shake**.

A cat tumbles from the top, rolling onto the carpet. It's a snore. A **huge** shuddering room-shaking snore. All the cats bare their claws and cling on for dear life.

Mr Tiblins is the ogre! He's the thing under all those cats.

'Pass the sticky tape,' whispers Nathan. He takes the straws out. He starts taping them together, making one long straw. Then he tapes a giant balloon to one end.

It's a Snore Catcher.

He passes it over to me. 'You go first,' he says.

I take a deep breath. Then I creep towards the cats.

The snore's finished. The cats are back on the mountain. And they're

all looking at me. Some of them are **hissing**. Oh dear. I don't think invisible ink works too well on cats.

I 'take another step forward. They're all hissing now. It's pretty scary. Loud too. I hope Mr Tiblins doesn't wake up.

'You're cleared for approach,' whispers Nathan.

Hand shaking, I start digging a tunnel through the cats. They don't like it much. Some of them start **SCRATCHING**. But I've got to keep going. We need the hot air.

And I'm through. I can feel Mr Tiblins's face. It's all sweaty and stubbly. I push the straw through the hole.

The cats are really angry now. They're hissing and yowling like crazy.

Surely Mr Tiblins is going to wake up? But wait! No! Here it comes! Another snore. As loud as an earthquake. The cats start scrabbling for a clawhold. Two of them tumble to the floor. It's the biggest snore in history. And I'm in place to catch it!

Hot stinky breath blasts my nostrils. It's disgusting but it's working! The balloon starts to fill.

'Don't let go!' shouts Nathan.

HISTORY CUP
WORLDS BIGGEST SNORE

MR TIBLINS

And I don't. I cling on tight. And suddenly I'm afloat! I'm off the floor. And on the ceiling!

'Pass the string!' I shout.

Nathan throws me the string. I tie it to the end of the balloon. I've caught the snore!

Nathan's turn. He tapes his balloon to the Snore Catcher. He starts his approach. And trips over a tabby cat. Down he tumbles – straight into the cat mountain.

'WHASS GOIN' AWN?!'

Mr Tiblins rises from the sofa. Cats go flying.

'*Go go go!*' shouts Nathan.

Mr Tiblins spins around. But he can't see us because we're invisible.

I start bouncing the balloon across the ceiling, towards the door.

'WHO'S IN 'ERE?!' screams Mr Tiblins.

He starts flinging cats at the balloon.

YOWL!

One pings off my elbow.

SCREECH!

One bumps off my knees.

I keep bouncing. Down the hall. Through the kitchen. And out the back door.

Mr Tiblins is right behind me. He's holding one more cat. A big fat ginger one. He takes aim. And flings it right at me.

But here comes Nathan. He leaps. And catches the cat! The cat looks grateful.

And so am I. I'm away! Off to Saurus Hill!

'Good luck!' shouts Nathan. 'Find that homework!'

I watch his floating head, fleeing Mr Tiblins's garden.

Team Dinosaur's down to one.

CHAPTER EIGHT
Saurus Hill

I'm flying! Higher and higher. Snore power really works!

Pretty soon the houses look like Lego blocks. There's my house. The one with the blue roof. Nathan's probably home already. I wish he was with me. Team Dinosaur's not supposed to be just me.

Here are the clouds. Big,

white and **fluffy**.

I wonder if they're *really* made of cotton wool. I reach up and grab one. Nope. Not soft enough.

And then everything goes white. I'm inside the clouds. I can't see any rain, though. Maybe this cloud's empty? Good thing too. Otherwise I'd be soaked.

And then I'm through. And there it is.

The top of Saurus Hill.

I'm the first person to ever see it! The trees are huge here. I've never seen anything like them. Their trunks are so **wide** you could build a house in them. And the bark's all

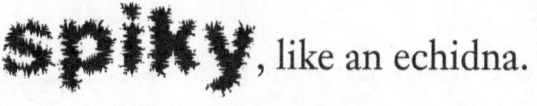 **spiky**, like an echidna.

But there's a problem. How do I land? I'm still going up. This snore is super strong.

I look down. And the answer appears. There's a safety pin holding up my pants (Bertie chewed my belt in two). If I make a hole in the balloon, I'll start going down.

I reach down and undo the safety pin.

Whoops. There go my pants. Down towards the trees.

Lucky I'm wearing clean underpants. I reach up and poke the pin into the balloon. Really, really slowly. I only want to make a small hole. Otherwise I'll fall too fast. And that might be scary.

Here I go. I push as slowly as I can.

And... **KAPOW!**

The balloon bursts with a bang.

Oh dear. I'm not going up anymore.
And I can't even flap. My wings dissolved
in the frog pond.

I start falling. **Faster** and **faster** and **faster** . Down towards the spiky trees. I think this is going to hurt.

WHAP!

I hit a leaf. It's enormous! The size of a paddling pool.

WHAP!

I hit another leaf.

WHAP WHAP WHAP

I bounce from leaf to leaf down through the trees.

And then . . .

61

FLOOMP!

I land on the forest floor. It's soft. Kind of spongy. And a good thing too. Otherwise it would have been

SPLAT!

I made it. I'm at the top of Saurus Hill. And look! There are my pants.

I pull them back on and use the balloon string as a belt. Lucky I hung onto that.

I stand up and look around.

This place is amazing. It's not just the trees. The flowers are huge too. So are the ferns. And. Whoa. Is that a centipede? I think it is. I quickly back away. The insects are **gigantic**.

I don't think this is a normal forest.

CHAPTER NINE
The Nest

I start walking. The huge trees rise up all around me. Thick, creepy vines wind around them, and purple flowers grow out of the trunks. And there are **spiderwebs** everywhere. Yuk.

It's really wet too. My clothes are soaked. I reckon the invisible ink will have washed off. Oh well. Invisible ink

probably doesn't work on pterodactyls anyway.

Every now and then I hear rustling in the bushes. But I don't see anything. I wonder what kind of animals live here?

And then I climb over a mossy tree stump and I see it. High up in a tree.

Homework!

Lots of it. All mixed up with leaves and sticks. It looks like some sort of nest.

A **really big**
nest. A pterodactyl-sized nest.

I start climbing up the tree. It's pretty tiring, but at least the spiky things on the trunk make good handholds. I'm getting closer and **closer** to the nest, although I can't see the pterodactyl. And that's good. Because visitors probably aren't welcome.

And then I notice something. A tickly feeling in my hands. Like something's crawling over them. I stop to look.

There *is* something crawling over them. Spiders. Hundreds and hundreds of giant spiders. Bright-red ones with black fangs. The whole tree is covered in them!

I climb up as quickly as I can and

66

leapfrog into the nest. I shake my arms and legs and head and everything, desperate to get the spiders off me. I hate spiders.

I look around me. I'm in a pterodactyl's nest. Awesome. It's really big. I reckon you could fit about six children in it. And it's kinda comfy. Although now's probably not the best time for a nap.

The nest is made of leaves and sticks and mud and vines. And homework. Why all the homework?

Because there's an egg in here. Wow. A real pterodactyl egg.

It's like a great big rock. And it's really **heavy**. I'm not sure a normal nest would work for an egg like this. It needs something tougher

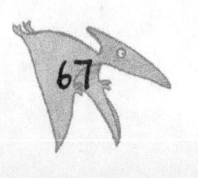

to keep it from falling. And there's nothing tougher than homework. We get special paper to do it on. And it's practically indestructible. But why build a nest so high up? Pterodactyls usually nest on the ground. (That's what Nathan says.)

No time to worry about that, though. I need to get moving. The pterodactyl will be back any moment. I look around. And there it is. My homework!

I'd recognise my drawings any-where because they're **brilliant**.

I grab it and start pulling. It's hard to budge, because there's all kinds of stuff stuck to it, but with a few sharp tugs the paper comes free. Hooray! I've got it!

68

It doesn't take me long to spot Nathan's homework. No-one else does algebra. I untangle it and put it in my pocket. And look. There's Susie's homework. I really like Susie. I bet she'd be glad to have it back. And surely one more won't hurt.

WHOOSH

A great black shape drops down from the treetops. I think my heart just **stopped**.

It's the pterodactyl.

I've been caught stealing from a pterosaur!

CHAPTER TEN
Dinner Time

The pterodactyl lands on the branch next to me. I **freeze**. It looks at the egg. And then it looks at me.

Whoops. This could be bad. The pterodactyl opens its beak. It's got big **SHARP** teeth. It's definitely a meat eater. And I think I'm about to be dinner.

But wait. Maybe not. What's it doing? The pterodactyl coughs. And something *flies* out of its mouth. It's a lizard. A big blue lizard.

The pterodactyl looks at me. Then it looks at the lizard. And then it waits. And that's when I realise pterodactyls aren't very clever. It must think I'm one of its babies.

And it wants me to eat the lizard.

I pick up the lizard. It's about as big as my arm. And it looks

disgusting

I look at the pterodactyl. Please don't make me eat this.

But the pterodactyl's not budging. I haven't got a choice. If I don't eat

the lizard, it'll know I'm not a baby pterodactyl. And then it might get

angry.

I close my eyes and open my mouth. I force myself to put the lizard between my lips. It's cold and clammy. Like raw fish. I think I'm going to be

sick. I take a deep breath. Then I take a bite.

BLEURGH! That tastes awful. Truly awful. Like cold spaghetti mixed with vegemite. And it's all **squishy**. Like jelly. But at least the pterodactyl's pleased. It nods its head, opens its wings and takes off again.

I cough out the lizard and use a finger to clean out my mouth. That was horrible. Time to get out of here.

But wait a second. There's Billy's homework. And Billy's cool. He'd be really pleased if I got it for him. It's tucked just behind the egg. If I can . . . just reach . . . round . . . and . . .

74

WHOOMP!

The pterodactyl's back. It opens its mouth and spits out something else. Must be dessert.

I take a look. This time it's a millipede. A big, **chunky**, sticky black millipede. It looks even nastier than the lizard.

The pterodactyl sits and waits patiently. I pick it up. The millipede is still alive. All its little legs are wriggling. No way. I can't eat this.

75

I put the millipede back down. But the pterodactyl doesn't like that. It squawks. Loudly. And takes a step closer. Oh dear. Refusal is not an option.

I pick up the **wriggly, squiggly** millipede and start lowering it towards my mouth. Every bit of my body is screaming at me not to do it. The millipede's not too keen either. It's arching its body away from me. I put it in my mouth and close my lips. I can feel it squirming against my tongue. I really am going to be sick.

I take a bite. It's the most horrible thing I've eaten. **Ever.** In my whole life. I'll never complain about carrots again. I wait for the pterodactyl to fly off, then I spit it out quickly. Poor millipede. It's not wriggling anymore.

Right. Let's get Billy's homework and go. It's trapped underneath the egg. I lean the egg to one side, grab the homework and pull.

And that's when the nest falls apart. Oops. I've taken too much homework.

I try to grab a branch but I'm not quick enough. I start to fall. Along with the sticks, the leaves and all the homework.

BANG ...

SLAP ...

SCRAPE . . .

I tumble through the branches and land on my bum on the forest floor. Ow. And then something heavy falls into my lap.

THUMP!

Ow, again.

I look at the thing in my lap. Oh. It's the pterosaur egg.

CHAPTER ELEVEN
The Egg Thief

I'm in big trouble now. I'm all alone, in a deep, dark forest, on top of a big, scary mountain. And I didn't even bring any snacks to eat. And there's no way of getting home. I haven't got any cardboard wings so I can't even try flapping.

And what's more, I've just adopted

a pterodactyl egg. A great big pterodactyl egg. And I'm not ready to be a mum. I'm only eight . . . and I'm a boy.

Stupid pterodactyl. Why did it build its nest so high up? All I took was a bit of homework. Why didn't it build its nest on the ground? You can't stick an egg like this in a tree nest. It's

too big.

Talking about homework, there's loads of it. All around me. The pterodactyl certainly was busy. I start picking it up and stuffing it down my pants. Just in case I do get home.

Suddenly there's a furious squawking from above me. It's the pterodactyl. She's just found out her nest isn't there anymore. And her egg is gone. She

doesn't sound too happy. She's trying to claw her way down through the branches. I think she knows her egg has fallen down here. But the branches and leaves are too thick.

I really should get this egg back to its mum. After all, it's my fault it fell. And I can't just leave it here. Who's going to look after it when it hatches?

But there's a problem. I can't climb back up the tree. Not with this egg. It's **too heavy**.

And the pterodactyl's too big to come down here and get it.

I'm going to have to find a clearing. Somewhere open so I can leave the egg for the pterodactyl to find.

I look around me. Tree trunks. That's all I can see. And ferns. And great big insects. I've no idea which way's which. I'll just have to guess.

I **spin** around three times with my eyes closed. Then I stop and open them. Guess what's in front of me? Tree trunks. Oh well. May as well go this way.

I start pushing my way through the undergrowth. It's hot and **scratchy**. And the egg is really heavy. It feels like my shoulders are going to fall off.

And then I hear a rustle. Off to my left. I stop and listen. Nothing. Just buzzing insects. I must have imagined it.

I keep walking. The trees are getting thicker. Not good. I don't think there are any clearings around here. This is a seriously thick forest.

Rustle. There it is again.

Something's following me. I'm sure of it. I stop and hold my breath. But I can still hear something breathing. I'm not alone.

I creep forward as quietly as I can. Tiptoe tiptoe tiptoe. *TRIP*. I fall over a tree root. Face first into the mud. Yuck. I push myself up and wipe the mud from my eyes. And that's when I see it.

There's a face. Peering at me from

between the leaves. It's got a curved beak and a round crest. But it's not a pterodactyl.

It's an oviraptor.

An egg thief!

Now I know why the pterodactyl built its nest so high.

CHAPTER TWELVE
The Great Chase

The oviraptor leaps out of the bushes and scratches at me with its foot. Its claws are curved and black. And big. One **SCRATCH** from them and I'm a goner.

I try to roll out of the way. But I'm not quick enough.

THUNK!

The oviraptor's claws sink into me. That's it. Game over. I must be bleeding all over the place.

Except I'm not. And I can't feel any pain either. That's odd. I take a look. I'm saved! The claws aren't wedged in me, they're wedged in someone's homework. I hope it's not mine.

I leap to my feet. Out comes the claw. I grab the egg and run.

The oviraptor's on my tail. I can hear it racing through the forest behind me. It lets out a deafening

SCREEEEECH.

It's a horrible noise. Like someone scraping fingernails down a blackboard. Is it screeching at me? No it's not. It's

screeching at something hiding in the trees. What's it screeching at?

That's what. Another face pokes out of the branches in front of me. Another oviraptor.

They're everywhere!

I make a sharp left turn, leap over a log and sprint for all I'm worth. And let me tell you, sprinting's not easy when you're carrying a pterodactyl egg.

There are two oviraptors on my tail now. They're about two metres tall and they've got feathers on their arms and legs. Oviraptors are weird-looking dinosaurs, but that doesn't make them any less vicious.

I think I'm losing them, though. That's one advantage of being small. It means I can slip between the trees

89

quicker. And I'm just thinking it might be safe to slow down a little bit when . . .

WOOOOAH!

I stop dead. I've come to the edge of a cliff. The cliff that goes all around Saurus Hill. And it's a huge cliff. One more step and I'd have gone over. With the pterodactyl egg.

I turn around. The oviraptors are right on top of me! I'm just about to get clawed!

I dive to my right. Oh no. I'm slipping! I desperately grab hold of a tree root. My feet are over the edge! I dig my fingers into the mud and drag myself back up. But the egg is about to roll off! I throw myself on top of it and trip up a lunging oviraptor. The

oviraptor screeches in terror as it *loses its balance* and falls over the cliff.

I pick up the egg and stand up. The second oviraptor's still there.

It's stock-still, waiting to strike. And it's got me backed up against the cliff.

It starts to walk towards me. It's not going to make the same mistake its friend did. It's going to do this slowly and make sure I don't get away.

I take a step back. I'm right on the edge now. There's nowhere for me to go. Sweat starts running down my forehead. I've run out of ideas.

There's no escape.

CHAPTER THIRTEEN
The Pterabike

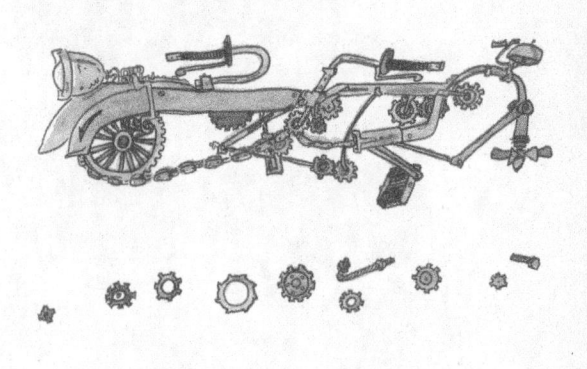

The oviraptor takes a step closer. I'm about to get **sliced**. I close my eyes. I can't look.

But hang on. Something's crashing through the forest, coming right towards us. It's making a dreadful noise. Maybe it's another oviraptor? Or something even bigger? Like a tyrannosaurus? But

no. It's . . . it's Nathan! On a bicycle!

He peddles straight towards the oviraptor. The oviraptor doesn't know what to do. It's never seen a bicycle before. Nathan lets outs a **blood curdling** yell. The oviraptor squawks with fear and disappears into the forest.

94

'Quick!' shouts Nathan. 'Into the basket!'

I don't need to be told twice. I jump into the basket attached to the front of the bike.

'Hang on!' screams Nathan. He's peddling straight towards the cliff edge. He's gone *bonkers!*

'Ready!' he yells. 'Goggles on!' He lowers a pair of goggles over his eyes. Then he hands me a pair. I put them on sharpish.

'Ger-onimo!' roars Nathan.

And we cycle straight off the cliff.

I scream. We're **tumbling** down towards the clouds. I'm going to die in a bicycle basket. And I'm not even wearing a helmet.

'Right,' shouts Nathan, 'let's get flapping!'

Get whatting? But then I look up. And I can't believe it! This isn't a normal bicycle. It's a *flying* bicycle!

Sticking out from the basket are two wings. Two magnificent wings. Made out of *wire* and some sort of cloth. They're enormous.

Nathan grabs a piece of string hanging down from the left wing. I grab the string hanging from the right wing. And then we start flapping.

flap flap flap flap flap
We flap like crazy. And the bike stops. It really does. It stops falling. 'Harder!' shouts Nathan. 'Use some elbow grease!'

I do. I really do. I flap until my arms ache.

And we start **climbing** up into the night sky. On a bicycle.

'Pretty nifty, eh?' says Nathan.

97

'It's amazing,' I say, and it is. 'How does it work?'

'It came to me while Mr Tiblins was chasing me with a shovel,' says Nathan. 'How do pterodactyls fly? I mean, they're enormous. It makes no sense. And then it hit me!'

'What, the shovel?'

'No, silly, the idea! Hollow bones!'

'What?'

'Pterodactyls. They've got hollow bones! That's why they're light enough to fly.'

'So?'

Nathan rolls his eyes. 'My bike. It's got a hollow frame! All I needed were giant wings, and hey presto – it's a pterabike!'

Nathan's really clever. I'd never have thought of that. 'What are the wings made out of?'

'The living-room curtains,' says Nathan. 'I was in a bit of a rush.'

'But Mum'll be **furious**.'

'She's already furious. How much angrier can she get?'

Fair point. We keep on flapping.

My arms are getting a bit tired.

'What do we do now?' I say.

'That depends,' says Nathan.

'On what?' I say.

'On that.' Nathan points up. It's the pterodactyl. And it's hovering right above us.

CHAPTER FOURTEEN
Revenge of the Oviraptor

The pterodactyl's **enormous**. Much bigger than us. It's going to knock us off our bike.

'What are you waiting for?' says Nathan.

I'm confused. What's he on about?

'*The egg,*' says Nathan. 'Give it the egg!'

Of course! I'd forgotten all about it. It's sitting on my lap in the basket. I reach down to lift it. But I'm not sure there's time.

Because it's hatching.

First it **shakes**. Then it **rattles**. Then a little crack appears in the side.

A tiny claw peeks out. Then another crack appears. Another claw. And then **CRRRACK**. The whole top comes off. And out pops a little head. With a crest, a beak and *tiny* little teeth. It's a baby pterodactyl.

'Wow,' I say. That's so cool. The

baby pterodactyl blinks and looks at me.
I reckon we're gonna be friends.

SQUAWK!

That's Mum. She sounds impatient.
I look up. She's flapping her wings and
looking at something. Something over
by the cliff.

SQUAAAAWK!

She doesn't just sound impatient.
She sounds worried. What's she looking
at?

'LOOK OUT!' shouts Nathan.

I look over at the cliff. We're about
level with the top of it now. And I see it,
just before it jumps.

It's the oviraptor. The one that
fell. It's been clinging on all this time,
waiting for us.

With a horrible *shriek*, the oviraptor leaps through the air and slams into the bike. The pterabike tips to the side. Nathan and I scream.

'LET GO OF THE EGG!' yells Nathan.

'But if I let go, the baby will die!' I shout back.

'TRUST ME! LET GO!' Nathan's flapping his wings, trying to knock the oviraptor off. But it's not working. It's clawing its way up the frame.

Oh well. Here goes nothing. I half-close my eyes and I let go of the egg. Down it falls. The oviraptor tries to grab it, taking one claw off the bike.

'HOLD ON!' shouts Nathan.

What's he going to do? WHOAAA! That's what. Nathan leans to one side. And flips the bike upside down. I fall out of the basket and just manage to grab the handlebars. I look down. Bad idea. It's a long, long way to the ground.

Nathan leans again, and the bike flips back up. And that's what does it. The oviraptor can't hold on. Not with one claw. It lets out an ear-splitting

shriek. And it falls. Down towards the clouds.

We're the right way up again. Time to start flapping. But there's a problem. The oviraptor's ripped a hole in one of the wings. Mum's curtains have had it.

'FLAP!' screams Nathan. 'FLAP LIKE CRAZY!'

And we do. We really do. But this time it doesn't work. The pterabike's busted.

We **plunge** towards the ground.

106

CHAPTER FIFTEEN
Handing in the Homework

I try to breathe. But I can't because I'm screaming too much.

WHOOSH!

We fall into the clouds. I can't see a thing. I keep on screaming.

WHEESH!

We come out of the clouds. And now I can see. I can see the ground, racing up towards us. I scream even louder. SWOOP!

Something huge sweeps underneath us.

THUMP!

Suddenly we're not falling anymore. We're sitting on something.

It's the pterodactyl. It's saved us. I peek over the pterosaur's side.

CRASH!

There goes the oviraptor. Into the trees far below.

The bike follows just after. But where's the baby?

SQUAWK!

It's a different squawk. More high-pitched. Nathan laughs. I look up, and there it is. The baby pterodactyl. Flying right next to our heads.

109

'Aren't pterosaurs awesome?' says Nathan. 'They can fly. Right out of the egg.'

Nathan's right. Pterodactyls are awesome.

'How did you know?' I ask him.

Nathan gives me his One Eyebrow Look. 'What do you mean, *how did I know?* I'm Captain. I know everything.'

I look around me. I'm *flying* in the night sky, on the back of a pterodactyl. It doesn't get any better than this.

'What now?' I say.

Nathan thinks for a moment. Then he grins. 'Perhaps it's time to hand in your homework.'

'There it is.' I point towards the house. It's thin, pointy and ugly. Just like its owner.

The pterodactyl circles, then lowers its claws and slams onto the roof.

CRACK!

A few roof tiles tumble into the garden.

'Wait for it,' says Nathan.

It doesn't take long. There's a scuffling sound from below. Someone scrambling out of bed.

'What on *earth* is going on?'

A window opens. And out pops a head. In hair rollers. And a nightcap.

'Miss Potts! Up here!' I put on my most innocent face.

Miss Potts turns her head.

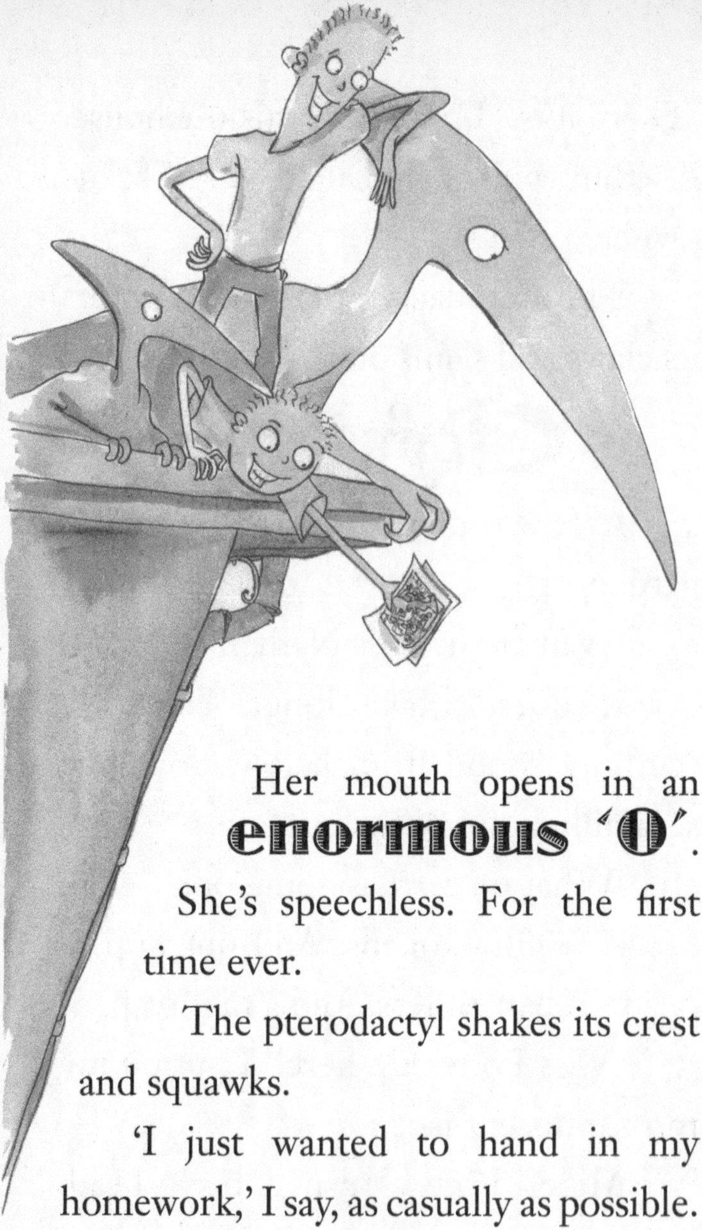

Her mouth opens in an **enormous 'O'**.

She's speechless. For the first time ever.

The pterodactyl shakes its crest and squawks.

'I just wanted to hand in my homework,' I say, as casually as possible.

I hop off the pterodactyl and walk down the roof.

Miss Potts stays **frozen**. Nathan stifles a giggling fit.

'After all,' I add, 'you did say I had to hand it in *before* class tomorrow.'

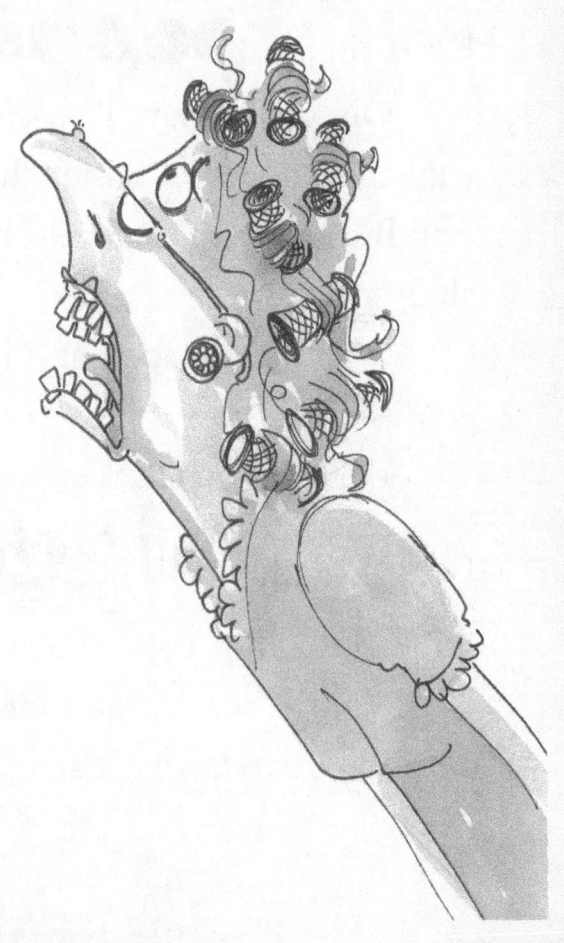

Miss Potts's mouth opens and closes. 'B . . . b . . . b,' she manages.

I reach into my pocket. And pull out my homework. It's a bit crumpled. But it'll do. I hand it to Miss Potts.

'G . . . g . . . g,' she mumbles. I think her brain just **popped**.

'Oh yes,' I say. I reach into my pants. 'And here's Susie's homework. And Billy's. And Wendy's.' I hand them all over.

Miss Potts gapes at me. Like a goldfish.

'Well, goodnight then, Miss Potts.' I give her my **biggest** smile. 'I do hope you sleep well.'

I climb back up the roof and jump onto the pterodactyl. It squawks again.

So does the baby perching next to it. The pterodactyl flaps its wings. And up we go.

'Nightie night, Pottsie,' shouts Nathan.

Miss Potts stares at us, her eyes bulging. We **soar up** towards the stars.

'Well,' says Nathan, 'I thought that went splendidly.'

I laugh out loud. I have a feeling school's gonna be a whole lot better this year.

CHAPTER SIXTEEN

Homework Heroes

I've just got home from school. Today was **a̱w̱ẹ̱s̱o̱m̱ẹ̱**.

Nathan and I were homework heroes. The pterodactyl stole loads of homework, and we saved almost all of it. The principal was so pleased that he gave the whole school Friday off. All because of us.

And as for Miss Potts, well, she was *very* nice to me. All day. I think she's scared I might visit her again in the middle of the night. Riding something **even bigger**. Like a diplodocus.

Of course, not everything's been perfect. Mum's not too happy about the curtains. Not one bit. But she *is*

happy about the phone call she got this morning from Miss Potts.

Sam's doing so well, said Miss Potts. *And I'm so sorry about the last call I made. And what a lovely boy Sam's become.* Mum told me all about it. I got the biggest hug ever.

But the best thing happened before school. I woke up and smelled something bad. Really bad. I got out of bed and there it was, sitting on my windowsill.

A dead, **smelly** bug. A big one.

I looked outside. But no-one was there. It didn't matter, though, because I knew that somewhere out there, someone very special was thinking about me. Two someones, actually.

I reckon Team Dinosaur's got two new recruits.

Although I'm still second in charge.

For more dinosaur-sized adventures, check out

Saurus Street 1: Tyrannosaurus in the Veggie Patch

AVAILABLE NOW!

Watch out for the next
two books in the

Saurus Street series

Publishing April 2013

Loved the book?

There's so much more
stuff to check out online